W9-BLG-550

SCOTT MAGOON

HARCOURT, INC.

Orlando Austin New York San Diego London

Requests for permission to make copies of any part of the work
should be submitted online at www.harcourt.com/contact or mailed
to the following address: Permissions Department, Harcourt, Inc.,
6277 Sea Harbor Drive, Orlando, Florida 32887-6777.

www.HarcourtBooks.com

Library of Congress Cataloging-in-Publication Data
Magoon, Scott.
Mystery Ride/Scott Magoon.
p. cm.
Summary: Three brothers never know where the surprise destination
will be when their adventurous parents announce "Mystery Ride!"
and the fivesome piles into the car for an outing.
[1. Automobile travel—Fiction. 2. Surprise—Fiction.
3. Family life—Fiction.] I. Title.
PZ7.M31266513My 2008
[E]—dc22   2007023481
ISBN 978-0-15-206021-3

First edition
H G F E D C B A

Printed in Singapore

To Mom and Dad—

thanks for the MANY mystery rides

The illustrations in this book were created digitally.
The display type was created by Scott Magoon.
The text type was set in Billy Serif.
Color separations by Colourscan Co. Pte. Ltd., Singapore
Printed and bound by Tien Wah Press, Singapore
Production supervision by Christine Witnik
Designed by April Ward

Sometimes when my parents gather my brothers and me into the car, we go to really fun places.

But on days like today, we ride along
for a few miles in happiness—

Now, a Mystery Ride may sound cool.

But it really means they're taking
us someplace we would never,
EVER want to go.

Today it was here.

Then, it got *really* bad.

When we finally got back into the car, Mom and Dad sensed our lack of enthusiasm.

So they tried to trick us . . . *again.*

But it wasn't.

Desperate for entertainment, we tried singing.

It passed the time.

At last, once all the mysteries were revealed, Dad took a familiar turn.

And just like that, we knew this Mystery Ride was about to get much better.

Mom and Dad say that sometimes it's good not to know where you're going and that getting there is half the adventure. The other half, Dad says, is getting your errands done.

Maybe he's right.
And maybe Mystery Rides
aren't so bad after all.

Especially when they end
with sprinkles on top.

THE END